A Note to Parents and Caregivers:

Read-it! Readers are for children who are just starting on the amazing road to reading. These beautiful books support both the acquisition of reading skills and the love of books.

 The PURPLE LEVEL presents basic topics and objects using high frequency words and simple language patterns.

 The RED LEVEL presents familiar topics using common words and repeating sentence patterns.

 The BLUE LEVEL presents new ideas using a larger vocabulary and varied sentence structure.

 The YELLOW LEVEL presents more challenging ideas, a broad vocabulary, and wide variety in sentence structure.

 The GREEN LEVEL presents more complex ideas, an extended vocabulary range, and expanded language structures.

 The ORANGE LEVEL presents a wide range of ideas and concepts using challenging vocabulary and complex language structures.

When sharing a book with your child, read in short stretches, pausing often to talk about the pictures. Have your child turn the pages and point to the pictures and familiar words. And be sure to reread favorite stories or parts of stories.

There is no right or wrong way to share books with children. Find time to read with your child, and pass on the legacy of literacy.

Adria F. Klein, Ph.D.
Professor Emeritus
California State University
San Bernardino, California

Editor: Christianne Jones
Designer: Nathan Gassman
Page Production: Tracy Kaehler
Creative Director: Keith Griffin
Editorial Director: Carol Jones
The illustrations in this book were created in pastels.

Picture Window Books
5115 Excelsior Boulevard
Suite 232
Minneapolis, MN 55416
877-845-8392
www.picturewindowbooks.com

Printed in the United States of America.

Library of Congress Cataloging-in-Publication Data
Syd's room / by Susan Blackaby ; illustrated by Frances Moore.
p. cm. — (Read-it! readers)
Summary: Syd has a hard time deciding what color she wants to paint her room.
ISBN 1-4048-1585-6 (hardcover)
[1. Color—Fiction.] I. Moore, Frances, ill. II. Title. II. Series.

PZ7.B5318Syd 2005
[E]—dc22
                                                              2005021454

Syd's Room

by Susan Blackaby
illustrated by Frances Moore

Special thanks to our advisers for their expertise:

Adria F. Klein, Ph.D.
Professor Emeritus, California State University
San Bernardino, California

Susan Kesselring, M.A.
Literacy Educator
Rosemount–Apple Valley–Eagan (Minnesota) School District

PiCTURE WiNDOW BOOKS
Minneapolis, Minnesota

4

Mom will paint Syd's room.
Syd will help.

Syd must pick a color.

What color will Syd pick?

Syd might pick red.

Her hair is red.

Syd might pick orange.

Her purse is orange.

Syd might pick yellow.

Lemons are yellow.

13

Syd might pick green.

Leaves are green.

Syd might pick blue.

The sky is blue.

17

Syd might pick purple.
Lavendar flowers are purple.

18

At last, Syd picks a color.
What color did Syd pick?

21

Syd could not pick just one color.
Syd and her mom painted a rainbow.

23

More *Read-it!* Readers

Bright pictures and fun stories help you practice your reading skills. Look for more books at your level.

Ann Plants a Garden 1-4048-1010-2
The Babysitter 1-4048-1187-7
Bess and Tess 1-4048-1013-7
The Best Soccer Player 1-4048-1055-2
Dan Gets Set 1-4048-1011-0
Fishing Trip 1-4048-1004-8
Jen Plays 1-4048-1008-0
Joey's First Day 1-4048-1174-5
Just Try It 1-4048-1175-3
Mary's Art 1-4048-1056-0
The Missing Tooth 1-4048-1592-9
Moving Day 1-4048-1006-4
Pat Picks Up 1-4048-1059-5
A Place for Mike 1-4048-1012-9
Room to Share 1-4048-1185-0
Shopping for Lunch 1-4048-1589-9
Wes Gets a Pet 1-4048-1060-9
Winter Fun for Kat 1-4048-1007-2
A Year of Fun 1-4048-1009-9

Looking for a specific title or level? A complete list of *Read-it!* Readers is available on our Web site:
www.picturewindowbooks.com

Sister Benedicta Ward read History at the Universities of Manchester and Oxford. A supernumerary Fellow of Harris Manchester College, she teaches Church History and Spirituality for the Faculty of Theology at the University of Oxford and is the Reader in the History of Christian Spirituality, with special interest in the Desert Fathers and Anglo-Saxon spirituality. Sister Benedicta is a member of the Anglican religious community of the Sisters of the Love of God, and has written a number of books on early monasticism and aspects of the Middle Ages.

IN THE COMPANY
OF CHRIST

Through Lent, Palm Sunday,
Good Friday and Easter to Pentecost

Benedicta Ward SLG

Benedicta Ward SLG

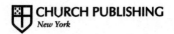

CHURCH PUBLISHING
New York

First published in Great Britain in 2005

Extracts from the Authorized Version of the Bible (The King James
Bible), the rights in which are vested in the Crown, are reproduced
by permission of the Crown's Patentee, Cambridge University Press.

Extracts from The Book of Common Prayer, the rights in which are
vested in the Crown, are reproduced by permission of the Crown's
Patentee, Cambridge University Press.

Every effort has been made to acknowledge fully the sources of
material reproduced in this book. The publisher apologizes for any
omissions that may remain and, if notified, will ensure that full
acknowledgements are made in a subsequent edition.

Church Publishing does not necessarily endorse the individual views
contained in its publications.

A catalog record for this book is available from the
Library of Congress

ISBN 0–89869–496–5

1 3 5 7 9 10 8 6 4 2

Church Publishing, Incorporated.
445 Fifth Avenue
New York, New York 10016

CONTENTS

*These pages are based on lectures given in
Canterbury during Holy Week 2004
by kind invitation of the
Dean and Chapter of Canterbury Cathedral,
and this book is therefore dedicated to them*

PREFACE

There are many occasions when people process: they take to the streets and walk together as a protest, for or against; they walk slowly for solemn events, whether it is for the coronation of a monarch or the burial of a child; they dance and sing and shout with joy in processions which are carnivals; they go together towards a special place in pilgrimage, religious or otherwise. In all these ways, it seems natural for people to want to be together and to be seen to be together, just walking, not doing anything except the fundamental action of a human being, walking upright. This affirmation of humanity is somehow enough, it says what cannot otherwise be expressed.

It can seem that Christianity is difficult and complex, that theology is distant, involved and maybe a bit boring, in fact quite beyond most people; but this is not what it is meant to be. The message of the gospel in the person of Christ is universal or it is nothing. This is not to diminish the work of professional theologians, who make proper use of God-given intellect by exercising it to the limits of their capacity on the revelation of God in Christ and wrestle to find words to communicate this to others; this is a vital part of Christianity, which is concerned with the Word and therefore with words. But it is possible also to come at Christianity from a rather different point of view, seeing it as something not too difficult but too simple for us, too basic, something to be apprehended therefore through the most simple thing that we all have – our bodies – by walking, by kneeling and bowing, by standing still. Humans tell stories, narratives, and go along together in order to focus the reality of their lives, to remember. People are not just brains, they have and indeed are bodies; so to apprehend truths they need to participate in events and make reality real for themselves. The cosmic event of the salvation of the world by God in Christ Jesus is a truth always present and it is for all – but we do not always live in the present. We have to find ways to wake up, to realize that ultimate truth is simple and for us. It is we who are complex and estranged, not God.

From the earliest times, Christians have had processions when they have done this kind of lived theology, and this has been especially true at the centre of the Christian year, the feast of Easter, when the redemption of mankind by the death and resurrection of Christ is annually celebrated. This pivotal moment has always been the subject of devotion and reverence as well as intense and far-reaching thought and analysis. Human beings, who are by their nature thinking creatures, want to extend their minds to the limits in trying to understand the work of God. For Christians, that kind of thinking is fundamentally done by analysis of doctrine based on the Scriptures.

But this should not make it seem that the Christian gospel of redemption is an intellectual problem for a select few when it is in fact a universal truth for all. The object of the subtleties of the theologians, there-fore, must be as accessible to the least intellectually alert as to the most complex mind, to a child as much as to a scholar. This can be expressed in the silences of prayer, where everyone is equal and this stillness before the mystery of God is an essential part of the Christian tradition. But Christians have instinctively also used their bodies created by God, not only by stillness but by actions, in understanding this re-creation of creation, and to do this they have simply walked together. They have done this notably during the days before the feast of Easter, in what came to be called 'Holy Week', and in this there have evolved three processions, on Palm Sunday, on Good Friday and on Easter night.

I have taken texts from the past, notably from the fourth century in Jerusalem and from the tenth century in England, not to make any point about the origins of these rituals but to show the continuity of this method of prayer, since they are virtually the same as those used today. They give us therefore friends along the way.

The great processions of Holy Week, however, are not isolated. Before them there are the 40 days called Lent and after them there are the 50 days of Pentecost. These can also be seen as part of a procession, a rainbow arc over the central treasure of Easter. Lent evolved in the first years of Christianity, partly as the time when those wanting to enter into Christian life were prepared for baptism at Easter, and Pentecost was seen as the days after baptism when the newly baptized began their Christian pilgrimage, from earth to heaven. It is possible to identify with both these processions: with Lent as the necessary preparation of ourselves each year for the great party of Easter, and Pentecost as the embodiment of the future pilgrimage that is all life. In each of these periods, it is not intellectual apprehension that matters most; there are here ways as simple and practical as those in the great processions, and also involving the body.

In order to give perspective to these ways of processing I have chosen to examine some earlier accounts of Lent, Palm Sunday, Good Friday, Easter and Pentecost. The main texts to be presented here are from an account of Holy Week in Jerusalem about AD 397, written by a nun, Egeria, from northern Europe who was there as a pilgrim and wrote home to her sisters about what she saw, thus providing the oldest account of Christian liturgy in Jerusalem.[1] The second group of texts is taken from the *Regularis Concordia: The Monastic Agreement*, compiled for English religious houses in the tenth century by Dunstan of Canterbury, Aethelwold of Winchester and King Edgar, showing similarities as well as changes of approach.[2] An Appendix has been added with early forms of hymns relating to all the times of the liturgical year which have been discussed; they contain remarkable theological insights set out in memorable and simple language and as such are useful for private meditation as well as for corporate use.

The picture on the cover is contemporary with the *Monastic Agreement* texts and is taken from a manuscript illumination in the *Benedictional of St Aethelwold*. The *Benedictional* was a book commissioned by Bishop Aethelwold of Winchester (963–984), a colleague of Dunstan of Canterbury, at the same time as the production of the *Monastic Agreement* and made by the same people. It is called on the first page 'this book of the advent of the Son of the loving Father'.[3] There is in the centre the open tomb with grave clothes suspended, to show they are empty. On the left are the sleeping soldiers, with swords and shields of no use. On the right are three women carrying three objects, presumably spices such as aloes and myrrh. Before the tomb the angel is seated, with one wing to earth, one wing to heaven, saying 'He is not here, he is risen.' The angel sits on an open book, seat or altar, indicating in visual form the word '*supersedere*': to sit above, to supersede. Christ has superseded all earthly means and is risen in new life for all. Crosses with flowers in each corner indicate the new paradise that is around and within, for resurrection joy belongs to heaven as well as earth.

What follows is an attempt to see the processions of this tradition as ways into the truth that is Christ, available for all, viable for all, and to suggest that anyone can experience them as part of the ultimate procession, that which is the dynamic life of the three persons of the Trinity.

> The meanest man in grey fields gone
> Behind the set of sun,
> Heareth between star and other star
> Through the door of the darkness fallen ajar,
> The counsel, eldest of things that are,
> The talk of the Three in One.[4]

Chapter 1

THE PILGRIMAGE
OF LENT

Lent, one of the oldest times of the year in the Christian Church, begins with a Sunday in the spring called 'Quadragesima Sunday', the beginning of 40 days; it is also called *Caput jejunium*, the head of the fast. What is it about? Is it a six-week period of repentance, of fasting, of giving things up? Is it a preparation for Easter? A commemoration of Christ's 40 days in the wilderness? Of Israel's 40 years in the desert? Is it a numerical calculation of infinitely involved permutations and significances, whose problems have been added to rather than simplified by the addition of the days from Ash Wednesday to Lent I, not to mention the complexities of Septuagesima, Sexagesima, and Quinquagesima Sundays? It can be all of these; it is a time with many and rich layers of meaning. I would like to consider some of these layers, and in peeling off the skins of the onion I hope to find a sweet and simple core, without discarding the skins in the process, and to see it as the beginning of pilgrimage with Christ.

First of all, the choice of the Gospel which is read on this first Sunday of Lent, about Christ in the wilderness (Matthew 4.1–11) seems to have been used consistently since the fourth century, though it is not the obvious piece of Scripture to choose for this period. However, it contains the number 40, and the commentaries of the Fathers, who delighted in numerical calculation and its significance, revolved a great deal around the significance of this number, to which was often added the number 50, for the following 50 days from Easter to Pentecost. As St Augustine says:

> The number ten . . . which pervades all life, enlarged four times, that is multiplied by the number which pertains to the body, makes the number 40; whose corresponding divisors added together make 50. For one and two and four and five and eight and ten, which are parts of the '40' number, added together make 50. Accordingly, the time in which we grieve and mourn is represented by the '40' number; the state of blessedness in which shall be our joy, is represented by the celebration of 50 days, that is from Easter to Pentecost.[1]

This may sound complex, but it is nothing compared to the nuances connected with the number 70, for the days from Septuagesima to Easter. And that is a simple affair when we consider the amazing convolutions of arithmetic and its meaning required in finding the date of Easter itself, and therefore of Lent, each year. Numerology seems today an abstruse affair; the use of arithmetic, the second means after writing by which people express and explore their world, is not popular when connected with religion, perhaps to our loss. Whatever it was for the ancients, and however entrancing in itself, it may not be our primary concern during these particular 40 days.

But the point Augustine was making about 40 and 50 introduces another aspect of Lent, perhaps more appropriate: Easter is here seen as the pivot between Lent and Pentecost, between mourning and joy, between Old and New Testaments. For centuries this link was explored through the arrangement of the public readings of the Bible during Lent; these were readings intimately linked, emerging from their solemn beginning in the pastoral concerns of the city of Rome and the processions each day of Lent to the papal station churches, to involve all Christendom. The sections read during Lent moved from Israel in the desert to Christ in the wilderness, from the story of the first creation towards the new creation, from the first Passover to the new Pasch. This was not the single yearly celebration by the early Church of an event out of time, but a drawn-out recapitulation of the history of salvation. The details of this sequence of readings have changed, but the central idea of linking Lent with the Scriptures remains. Moreover, this linking through Lent and Eastertide of Old and New Covenants was, by the ninth century at least, given expression on Easter night both by a recapitulation of the readings of Lent, and by the visual image of a procession coming out of the darkness of Adam cast out of Eden to the new banquet of the redeemed, led like Israel in the desert, by the light and the cloud of the paschal candle. This image of the 40 days linked to the 40 years as the pilgrimage of the new Israel, both in Lent and through life, is still most deeply sensed; and the great Welsh hymn, 'Guide me, O thou great Redeemer', exactly reflects such an understanding. Guided by God through 'this barren land', we go through the desert of this life as Israel was led out of captivity. For us also, 'the fiery, cloudy pillar' of God's presence leads us. We are fed by the 'bread of heaven', which is no longer manna but the 'true bread that comes down from heaven', and with the water of baptism from the side of Christ on the cross, fulfilling the type of the 'crystal fountain' of water struck from the rock by Moses. We are led no longer to 'the verge of Jordan' and 'Canaan's shore', but to the great stream of death, the way into the new heaven and earth. John Hughes's great music aptly sets off the magnificence of the words of William Williams with their ancient sense of the spiritual and moral meanings of the Scriptures: such a hymn suggests that this typological approach is by no means out of date (see Appendix).

As well as the numerical and scriptural aspects of Lent, it is often proposed that Lent should be filled with the remembrance of the two ways in which it was used in the early Church: for the preparation of candidates for the great moment of baptism at Easter, and for the equally serious preparation of the public penitents, who during these days from Ash Wednesday anticipated their no less public reconciliation. These two aspects of Lent in themselves hardly affect us, and in fact must have soon ceased to have their original significance. To pray one's way through Lent alongside the last preparations of catechumens for baptism, for instance, has a somewhat anachronistic air. It must have happened that in the fourth century the large numbers of candidates for baptism soon diminished; after the peace of the Church there was clearly no longer a large number of unbaptized adults, but instead congregations of believers. Again, Lent alongside the public sinners, the excommunicate preparing for public reconciliation, has also a fanciful air about it. The system of public penance was long ago replaced by private reconciliation, excommunication by a more personal and private repentance. But Lent can indeed still be seen as a pilgrimage towards Easter, with thoughts of baptism and repentance always before us as well as already accomplished, though perhaps now these historical layers must bear a more interior meaning. But it is as baptized Christians that we now approach Lent. Already in the fourth century, Lenten sermons put the stress not on preparation for baptism or for reconciliation, but on Lent as a special time for baptized Christians to be with Christ in the wilderness, to begin to be what they already are by baptism. St John Chrysostom was very clear on this point:

When the Lord had been baptized in water by John, he was then led by the Spirit into the desert . . . Not alone is Christ led by the Spirit into the desert, but so likewise are all the sons of God who have within them the Holy Spirit. The temptations of the devil are specially directed against those who have been sanctified.[2]

How then is the mature, established, baptized Christian to experience Lent? The theme most usually associated with Lent today is not arithmetic, typology, baptism or forgiveness; Lent is often reduced to being what it is called in the liturgy – *jejunium*, the fast. Moreover, this is most often seen as a chance to pull oneself together, to make resolutions; to do something, however small, with a rather Pelagian understanding of self-discipline and almsgiving. It is customary to speak of penance, fasting, doing without, a time of unusual effort, with a corresponding failure and consequent gloom. Dr Pusey, one of the leaders of the Oxford Movement, preaching at Christ Church on the first Sunday in Lent in 1875, was particularly severe with the undergraduates before him in this matter of the use of Lent to emphasize serious Christian commitment:

> You who are here today profess by your being here that you do not belong to these classes of the proud and sensual, and yet I fear there is hardly a law of God, scarcely a word of our Redeemer, which if you look it in the face, see what it means, what it requires of you, you could pretend to yourselves that you were even in the way of keeping it.[3]

He classed his congregation of young undergraduates, perhaps too flatteringly, all things considered, with 'a certain poor heathen', by whom he meant one of the major theologians of the Church, Augustine of Hippo, writing in his *Confessions* about his attitude before his baptism:

> He was a heathen when he made a heathen prayer and knew not God; probably it is the one prayer for those who neglect to turn to God now . . . It is that raven cry, 'O Lord, make me chaste, only not yet.'[4]

In another sermon on 'lukewarmness', he left the parallel with Augustine of Hippo behind and begged the same young men, in impassioned terms, to begin

> well-regulated fasting by forgoing one material self-indulgence which was absolutely unknown forty years ago and if forgone would feed Christ in some thousands in whom he is an hungered: that is, your cigars.[5]

This abstinence may not be so demanding now as it was then, when cigars had only fairly recently reached England from Cuba after the British campaign there in 1810, but at least the students were urged to do something both possible and practical. The effect, as well as being mildly comic for us, is also deplorably negative. It is unfortunate, to say the least, that Christians so often give the impression of just giving up, of being *against* life and joy and *for* misery and loss. No serious-minded man would suppose that Christian life and its epitome as expressed in <u>Lent</u> can be easy, but because it is a serious matter <u>it does not have to be a gloomy one. We are not pretending in Lent that Christ is not risen from the dead; the light of Easter shines through the whole of Lent so that it is a bright season, of lightness, of running the race that is set before us, looking unto Jesus.</u> The Anglo-Saxons, for all their enthusiasm for Roman ways, stubbornly and without argument preserved this sense by their use of the words 'Easter' and 'Lent', words with a different connotation from the universal *Pascha* and *Jejunium*. Easter they took from Eostere, goddess of spring; and Lent was their word for spring itself. This sense of life and energy about Lent seems vital in our approach to these 40 days. 'Now God be thanked', we might say with the poet Rupert Brooke who was commenting on a different battle, 'who has matched us with his hour . . . as swimmers into cleanness leaping'.[6]

While aware of the rich layers of numerology and scriptural exegesis, of the rites of baptism and reconciliation, of the asceticism of fasting and almsgiving, nevertheless we now look forward and not back. 'Not what thou art, nor what thou hast been seeth God with his merciful eyes, but what thou wouldst be', says the author of *The Cloud of Unknowing*.[7] <u>Lent is no romantic reflection on the past but a moment of eager adventure now.</u> The Venerable Bede exclaimed, 'Behold, this wondrous and most profitable time of our Pasch is now approaching.'[8] <u>Lent for Christians is not an imaginary and depressing replay but the whole</u>

serious and glorious matter of salvation. The point of the Gospel reading on this day is not to show a past event of Christ, baptized by John and then led into the desert by the Spirit of God, where he was with the angels and the animals, alone for 40 days, and fed by the word of God, then tempted suddenly, awfully, at the end. The man Christ Jesus is Adam, is ourselves, outside Eden, in the desolation he has made, receiving there the new gift of redemption. This desert experience, the solitude for the 40 days of aloneness before God, of living at the limits of human existence, near to the beasts and angels, has a central importance for us. This response with delight to the opportunity Lent gives to know ourselves in the silence of God is found particularly in the literature of early Christian monasticism. When St Benedict said that the life of a monk is always Lent,[9] he means that condition is a privilege, not a bore. Anselm called it *pondus cantabile*, a burden to be borne singing.[10]

I will take one instance of this 'wondrous and most profitable time' from the earliest records of the Christian monastic tradition.[11] It is a story from the desert about a very good man and a very bad woman. Zossima, the good man, was a well-educated monk; in fact, he had reached a point in his life where he believed he could not find anyone more good and clever than himself. On the first day of Lent, he went out, as did the rest of the community, to spend the 40 days alone in the Judaean desert. As he walked along on his own he saw a shadow out of the corner of his eye, and following it he met Mary, a former prostitute

11

from Alexandria. He was the first human being she had seen for 47 years. She told him her story, an account of consistent and eagerly chosen lust, the pattern of the easy choices of all humankind, and of the equally dramatic change of heart that came to her in the Holy Sepulchre in Jerusalem by the simple discovery that you can't have everything; that what you have made yourself is what you are. On that momentous day she had found that she could not enter and venerate the True Cross with the pilgrims. Shocked to the centre of her soul, she sought no counselling, no confession, no after-care, no instruction, no sacraments or good works; she immediately took herself into the desert, crossing the Jordan. She then lived alone in all the anguish of reality before God. When Zossima heard her story he wept not for her but for himself, seeing his self-righteous efforts at discipline for what they were: attempts to buy Christ, whose only joy is the heart broken open towards the freedom of his love. And so he saw the sinful woman coming towards him by the fitful light of the moon, and she was walking lightly on the waters of the river.

Perhaps this glimpse of the wilderness shows that Christ is too plain for us, that the gift of God is not complicated but utterly simple. Though Lent could be approached through numerology, baptismal images, echoes of penitence, fasting, almsgiving and especially the Scriptures as the way into Easter, they have meaning only when discovered in a stillness that is quiet enough and simple enough to enable us to receive God as a gift.

To enter into silence could, of course, be the reverse of life giving; there are some silences which are negative and destructive. But the true stillness of the wilderness is not idleness or contempt: it is an entry into another kind of converse, to know yourself within the light of the mercy of God. It can remind us that there is always a need to refrain from reliance on our busy activities and works. The praying man has to stand back, in order to let God be God and to be known by him, and this is our desert. There is the parallel need of any scholar at any stage to be silent before the text and let it be itself in its context and speak, and that also is our desert. The fact of Lent underlines this permanent need; this stillness poises us to receive the gift called insight, the space needed for thought and deep consideration, when we can be free for the night of understanding. Truth I suppose to be our aim, and perhaps the hardest truth to know and to communicate is the fact that talking and writing is not the great matter we think it, unless it is held within the vast stillness of God. This knowledge out of silence is not an easy way to know truth, but for it we have the greatest Exemplar of all. As Guigo the Carthusian puts it, 'Without form or comeliness, weak and nailed to a cross, thus is Truth known.'[12]

These themes were recognized in Jerusalem in the fourth century by the pilgrim Egeria, who observed the keeping of Lent there and wrote home to tell her sisters about it, stressing what would be new to them. She noticed that there was in Lent an increase in the number of services and processions, with singing,

which were there not as something imposed but
because they were wanted. This was not so different
from the life her sisters knew in Lent at home but
there was a new detail which was a pastoral one:
everyone who could, would arrive eagerly on each of
the 40 days at the central church in order to understand better what was to happen later:

> During Lent the bishop preaches daily; his subject
> is God's law; during the forty days he goes through
> the whole Bible, beginning with Genesis and relat-
> ing the meaning, first literally and then spiritually.
> Thus all the people in these parts are able to follow
> the scriptures when they are read in church.[13]

The basis was the Bible, explained simply, and it is
clear that this preaching was not a passive affair:

> At ordinary services when the bishop sits and
> preaches, ladies and sisters, the faithful utter excla-
> mations but when they come to hear him explaining
> during Lent, their exclamations are far louder, God
> is my witness, and when it is related and interpreted
> like this, they ask questions on each point.[14]

Egeria goes on to describe the way in which people
she observed in Jerusalem fasted during Lent, and this
was characterized by personal choice and an eager-
ness to do all one can; it is assumed that all will want
to do as much as possible, but there is no external rule
imposed:

For fasting during Lent, there are some who eat nothing during the whole week, others have a meal half way through the week, others eat on two days in the week, some have a meal each evening. No one lays down how much is to be done but each person does what he can; those who keep the full rule are not praised and those who do less are not criticised.[15]

By the tenth century in England, the observance of Lent in a monastery was more formal, and the details given in the *Monastic Agreement* are about more corporate prayers and processions. Here, the beginning of Lent was marked by a ceremony, which is still carried out, of putting a mark of ash on the forehead of each participant as a reminder of the earth from which we were made, the humility of being as ash before the Lord. In the *Monastic Agreement*, Lent began with this exterior and physical act of humility: 'On Ash Wednesday when *Nones* has been sung, the abbot wearing a stole shall bless the ashes and shall then lay the blessed ashes on the head of each brother.'[16] Fasting was then expected by all and was regulated for a large community, but some choice was still left to each one:

The bell shall be rung for vespers and there shall be a space for prayer. Then in the interval while the bells are ringing, those who wish shall partake of the mixtum [a meal], those who do not wish to shall have permission to forgo it . . . On these holy days of Lent there shall be some increase in divine worship . . . whereby being freed from the bonds of sin we may rise to heavenly things by the steps of the virtues.[17]

In both these accounts, people were eager for Lent, and saw it as a way of processing in heart towards God; and in both cases, silence was needed as well as company. History is full of moments of the silent reality before God that comes within the desolations of such pilgrimage. They have always issued into glory. The classic seventeenth-century account of Christian life, *The Pilgrim's Progress*, using the imagery of pilgrimage, concludes with some words that contain most of all that sense of a serious but eagerly chosen pilgrimage through 'this barren land' of life and of Lent, to the verge of Jordan and Canaan's shore, in company but also in silence, with the underlying truth that such pilgrimage is not darkness and then light, but a wilderness which is always blossoming in resurrection:

Then said Mr Valiant-for-Truth: I am going to my Father's; and though with great difficulty I have got hither, yet now I do not repent me of all the troubles that I have been at to arrive where I am.

Mr Standfast said: I see myself now at the end of my journey, my toilsome days are ended. I am going to see that head which was crowned with thorns and the face which was spit upon for me . . . He has held me, and hath kept me from mine iniquities; yea, my steps hath he strengthened in his way.

The last words of Mr Despondency were, Farewell night; welcome day! His daughter, Much-Afraid, went through the river singing, but no one could understand what she said. But glorious it was to see how the upper region was filled with horses and chariots, with trumpeters and pipers, with singers and players on stringed instruments, to welcome the pilgrims as they went up, and followed one another in at the beautiful gate of the City.[18]

Chapter 2

PALM SUNDAY

The pilgrimage of Lent takes on a new dimension with Palm Sunday, the beginning of Holy Week. In the Gospels, the entry of Christ into Jerusalem is seen as the beginning of his Passion, but at first in the early Church it was not regarded as a separate event. In the earliest years of Christianity, the great mystery of salvation was apprehended as one single cosmic event called Jesus Christ; his return to the Father with our humanity was central at every point, whether it was the martyr saying, 'I am the wheat of Christ, let me be ground by the teeth of beasts that I may be found pure bread'[1] or Christian worshippers in private houses, or in the catacombs, saying, 'Let grace come and this world pass away; amen, come, Lord Jesus'.[2] But in the fourth century, with the peace of the Church, there was a change; the places and the individual events of the Gospel came to matter much more.[3] There was a need to tell a story, to walk to a place, to stand under in order to understand. One expression of this is that from the fourth century until today, Christians have created things to do together, rituals, in order to experience for themselves the great simplicity of redemption. These rituals are meant to recur, they are the stones of an archway which, once built, is there to use, to go in and out by prayer and so to find pasture. We do not want to be rebuilding a different-shaped arch, however entrancing, but to use what we have, what we are used to, in order to enter into the real business of prayer. So the ceremonies of Holy Week, beginning with Palm Sunday, are there to be used, and this is a physical matter, a use of the body, so that all of ourselves will know. Intellectual apprehension of truth is all very well, and indeed for some it is enough; but for most of us, we live in a half-light, neither awake nor asleep, wanting to understand but not quite able to think it through; we need to be there to act it out, to participate. This is in no way an alternative or lesser kind of theologizing; by both ways we come to the central theme of redemption, the flesh-taking of Christ in which he returns to the Father and takes us into the dynamic life of the Trinity which is the ultimate procession, and it is by physical processions that we can learn to become part of that reality.

The last days of Holy Week provide a simple way of allowing the body, the flesh, to learn theological truth by doing and being in earthly processions. Palm Sunday's procession is about how to do the basic human thing – to walk, to take one step, just to be able to do the next step, and to remain with that doing, not seeing a much quicker way to get there by a bus, a train, a ship, a plane, which are quicker than our feet; we are always dashing through in order to be some-where else, and when we are there then we think we will begin. But the procession is a slow, corporate event, the pace set by the weakest and slowest. Like growing, a procession is something done for its own sake, and in doing it we are becoming what we are not, going by a way we do not understand, for a purpose that is God's, not ours, in ways that are too simple for our sight. We will never of course be ready on earth for the full 'procession' which is the dynamism of the life of love which is the Trinity, since we are broken human beings, with limited sight; but given our consent, God can lead us by the flesh he created, to understand and apprehend the image of God which he placed within us. All that is needed is to give a minute assent, however impatient and grudg-ing, and then just to do it. A procession can be seen as a sacrament, 'an outward and visible sign of an inward and spiritual grace'. In the same way that we read *through* the letter of the Scriptures to the inner truth, so we understand more by walking than we know; it is the work and gift of God.

Meditation upon the processions of Holy Week is rightly undertaken at its commencement. In the early Church, for the first three days of Holy Week, on Monday, Tuesday and Wednesday, the custom was to have only plain readings from Scripture; later, what was read each day were the separate accounts of the Passion. Then as now, these were days of stillness and silence when all were to be prepared, emptied, turned

23

towards the Saviour's great work. After the signs we gave ourselves during Lent of being ready to become empty by giving things up and therefore more free, now that desire will be put to the test. There is nothing now to be done or thought. It is the end of Lent, the pause before the great mystery of Redemption. In this pause, it is possible to reflect on these three processions, on Palm Sunday, Good Friday and Easter night, as ways into the great procession which is the life of Trinity, and this is not just for ourselves here and now. First, we walk with so many others from the past, joined with them by our present actions. We receive life from the hands of the dead to live it out ourselves and pass it on to others, and that is true tradition. We are walking with our friends. And second, we do not do this for ourselves only, but for the whole of creation; insofar as one small portion of humanity which is us assents to the love of God, so the whole of creation becomes part of redeeming work.

To find our friends in this procession of love, I suggest we look in two places which have been opened to us during Lent: first in the early Church, in the earliest accounts of Holy Week which come from the visit to Jerusalem of the Spanish nun, Egeria,[4] writing at the end of the fourth century. Then, we can see how these events were re-enacted in England, in Winchester and in Canterbury, in the Middle Ages.[5] Here, like Egeria and the monks of Winchester, we will walk with the unbaptized, the catechumens; then kneel with the penitents; then stand with the baptized.

24

So I suggest that we recall first of all that we are creatures before the Creator. We are with those preparing for Easter, that is the catechumens, the unbaptized, those who have so far only assented to going this way. The context of the biblical account of Palm Sunday suggests that our place is here. In the Gospel according to St John, the account of the entry into Jerusalem is followed by the inclusion of the foreigners, the Greeks, ourselves:

> There were certain Greeks among them that came up to worship at the feast: The same came therefore to Philip ... and desired him, saying, 'Sir, we would see Jesus'. Philip cometh and telleth Andrew: and again Andrew and Philip tell Jesus. And Jesus answered them, saying, 'The hour is come, that the Son of man should be glorified. Verily, verily, I say unto you, Except a corn of wheat fall into the ground and die, it abideth alone: but if it die, it bringeth forth much fruit.' (John 12.20–24)

We are with the Greeks, and we also say, 'Sir, we would see Jesus', that is his glory and this is our request all the days. 'The hour is come' for the glory of Jesus when we bring ourselves; or, like Andrew and Philip, we bring others, brothers or strangers, with us, knowing blindly that this is the answer to all desires. Jesus uses the same phrase later about his death and speaks of it in connection with his glory: 'the hour is come', the hour of death and life. The image he uses, of the seed falling into the ground and dying, is one which would be

25

familiar to any Greek from their own mysteries; God always begins where we are. There is no new creation without the first. We have to come to the place where we know who we are. This feast affirms the goodness of creation: to be who you are. There is here a great sense that creation is good; St Benedict saw creation in a ray of light, given beauty from God.[6] Julian of Norwich saw creation as a hazelnut, nothing in itself, but with a wonderful reality 'because God loves it'.[7] It is such truths as these that we can begin to understand by the procession of Palm Sunday.

1. The procession on Palm Sunday

[They] took branches of palm trees, and went forth to meet him, and cried, 'Hosanna: blessed is the King of Israel that comes in the name of the Lord.' And Jesus, when he had found a young ass, sat thereon. (John 12.13–14)

The earliest account of a Palm Sunday procession comes from Egeria, the nun from Spain or Gaul, who visited Palestine as a pilgrim in the fourth century, between 381 and 384. She wrote in Latin, and only one manuscript of her writing survives: this was discovered in a poor state of preservation with some pages missing and published in 1887.[8] There are references to her elsewhere, and it is from those that we learn her name. Eagerly visiting places in Palestine connected with both Old and New Testaments, she wrote home to her sisters describing her adventures, and she was especially keen to tell them what was new in Holy Week in Jerusalem; this gives us, as well as her sisters, a unique view of what Holy Week was like in Jerusalem in the fourth century. She wrote:

On Sunday, at one o'clock the people go up to the Eleona[9] church on the mount of Olives . . . At five o'clock the passage is read from the Gospel about the children who met the Lord with palm branches, saying, 'Blessed is he that comes in the name of the Lord.' At this the bishop and all the people rise from their places, and start off on foot down from the summit of the Mount of Olives. All the people go before him with psalms and antiphons, all the time repeating, 'Blessed is he that comes in the name of the Lord.' The babies and the ones too young to walk are carried on their parents' shoulders. Everyone is carrying branches, either of palm or olive, and they accompany the bishop in the very way the people did when once they went down with the Lord. They go on foot all down the Mount to the city, and all through the city to the Anastasis [the tomb of Christ in the Martyrium, the great new church of Constantine and Helena] but they have to go gently on account of the older women and men among them who might get tired. So it is already late when they reach the Anastasis; but even though it is late they hold Lucernarium [the blessing of the evening lamps] when they get there, then have a prayer at the cross, and the people are dismissed.[10]

There is a procession here but it is not very organized, not very fast, and the participants are careful about all involved. They are making use of having the actual place there. They are carrying what plants were there, that is palms and olive branches. The bishop represents Christ in humility and in triumph, the people are following, as the account says the Jews did, with enthusiasm after the raising of Lazarus. For each this is a physical statement of being ready to go with him. It's a party, informal, with care for the reality of youth and age and weakness. The fact of being there in this first mysterious event was enough.

2. *Anglo-Saxon Palm Sunday* (Regularis Concordia) *c. 970*

Processions were important in the first coming of the missionaries to Anglo-Saxon England in 597, and when Augustine came to Canterbury bringing the gospel to the Anglo-Saxons he came walking with others, carrying a silver cross as well as an icon of the face of Jesus; they came in the spring and in procession:

> Augustine and his companions came to meet King Aethelberht; endowed with divine not devilish power and bearing as their standard a silver cross and the image of our Lord and Saviour painted on a panel. They chanted litanies and uttered prayers to the Lord for their own eternal salvation and the salvation of those for whom and to whom they had come ... and the king gave them a place in Canterbury ...[11]

Processions began Christian life in England, in association with royalty, and when in 970 there was a record made of the standard rituals observed in English monastic houses, it was done under the guidance of Dunstan of Canterbury and Aethelwold of Winchester in alliance with King Edgar. It contained an account of a Palm Sunday procession, certainly used in Winchester but very probably in Canterbury also when the cathedral was again a monastery; two of the oldest tenth-century manuscripts of the *Monastic Agreement* were made in Canterbury with notes for their use.[12]

On Palm Sunday . . . the greater procession shall take place and it shall be held thus: the brethren vested in albs if this can be done and the weather permits shall go to the church where the palms are, silently, in order of procession and occupied with psalmody . . . On reaching the church . . . the gospel, 'A great multitude' is read by the deacon as far as the words 'Lo, the whole world is gone after Him'. The blessing of the palms follows. After the blessing, the palms shall be sprinkled with holy water and censed; when the children begin the antiphon 'the children of the Hebrews' the palms shall be distributed . . . then the greater antiphons shall be intoned and the procession shall go forth, singing 'All glory laud and honour, to thee redeemer king, to whom the lips of children, do sweet hosannas sing' (Theodulf of Orleans, +821) with its verses [see Appendix]. The cantor on reaching the church shall intone 'When the Lord entered into the city' and the doors shall be opened; when all have entered they shall hold palms in their hands until the offertory has been sung.[13]

This is more organized but still out of doors with palms; since it is England, there are also flowers, and it is necessary to say: 'weather permitting' – the same readings, the same simple actions; and there is always this element of the children, of being the lowest and least important. The 'children of the Hebrews' were not initially children as such, but this was a synonym for the Hebrew people; the fact of children being present with their parents in fourth-century Jerusalem and again in medieval England as choirboys, suggested that children was meant in the text. There is here also a crowd of friends, all prepared to just walk with the body so that the spirit may respond. These were not especially good, pious or clever people; illuminations show them as the citizens of Jerusalem, Gentiles and Jews, not as apostles or disciples; and in fact there was one friend among them, at the centre of that procession, who was not even human, but who is central in all pictures of the procession. Perhaps he is our best friend, since he was realistically seeing himself as nothing whatever except for the moment of being with Jesus:

> When fishes flew and forests walked
> And figs grew upon thorn
> Some moment when the moon was blood

Then surely I was born.
With monstrous head and sickening cry
And ears like errant wings,
The devil's walking parody
On all four-footed things.
The tattered outlaw of the earth,
Of ancient crooked will,
Starve, scourge, deride me: I am dumb,
I keep my secret still.
Fools! For I also had my hour;
One far fierce hour and sweet:
There was a shout about my ears
And palms before my feet.[14]

Sometimes a donkey is introduced into modern Palm Sunday processions, though I have never heard of an archbishop riding on one, but this can become a distraction; we are not here to be amused by a dear little animal or by sweet, small children around it. That is all very well, but the significance of the ass is twofold: it is a sign that Christ enters Jerusalem and therefore our own souls, as the Prince of Peace; and there is the meaning of the ass as our fleshly nature, used by Christ in his flesh-taking, what Langland called, 'a horse named flesh – I took it from mankind'.[15] The '*pueri hebororum*' also were not kiddies; the phrase is a euphemism for 'Jews'. It is so easy to look only on the physical, outside event and miss the inner significance. In actions, as well as in reading, it is necessary to look below the surface to truth within.

The earliest record, then, of Palm Sunday is of a simple outdoor procession with branches, of all kinds of people, taking care of each other, learning to walk together, whether they liked each other or not, following the plain words of the Gospel as they went towards Jerusalem, learning physically how to continue to seek the Jerusalem above that is free. And 500 years later, there was the same basic commitment to walk in this way. A thousand years from then, for us there is the same pattern. There is no need to think we cannot do this if we are unable to go to Jerusalem. It is the Jerusalem which is above that we seek. Each church is a Jerusalem, the maze in a cathedral is a path to Jerusalem, the vision of peace. It is not only a particular hillside that is to be sought, but because a particular hillside was once chosen we now seek to go that way wherever we can, for the catastrophic moment of commitment to something we don't yet understand. The physical place is not what matters; as Jerome said, 'It is praiseworthy not to have been in Jerusalem but to live well for Jerusalem.'[16] We do what we can where we are; we are children, we are catechumens, we are the Jewish people, we are donkeys. Ours is an uncomplaining assent to the mystery of the mighty work of God done in Christ and established in us for the whole of creation:

> Where Thou leadest I would go,
> Walking in Thy steps below,
> Till before my Father's Throne
> I shall know as I am known.[17]

Chapter 3

GOOD FRIDAY

The procession on Palm Sunday fittingly begins the Christian celebration of Holy Week, as it is the beginning of the Passion of Christ as described in the Gospels. With the next stage in the Passion, there is another procession, and again it is a procession in which we use our bodies to teach us about life and death in the body of Christ. There we walked; here we kneel or bow down. We are following the way of the cross in discipleship. What does it mean, 'to follow'? Two things at least: it means, first, to walk in the footsteps of Jesus the man of Galilee, to see what he saw. In the thirteenth century, the Franciscans in Jerusalem introduced the custom of walking the 'Stations of the Cross'[1] along the route Christ took carrying his cross to Golgotha, pausing at 14 places to remember aspects of that procession. This method of stirring the soul to repentance by imagining the details of Christ's suffering seems to have been started two centuries earlier by Anselm, Archbishop of Canterbury (1033–1109) in his very influential prayers and meditations; there, in his 'Prayer to Christ', he meditates on the details of the pain of the cross, imagining himself there, to make himself understand the price of salvation and his responsibility for it:

I am mindful of your passion
your buffeting, your scourging, your cross,
    your wounds,
how you were slain for me . . .[2]

This method of using the details of the suffering of the human Jesus to arouse compunction was expanded to include the whole route to the cross, and this 'way of the cross' has had a distinguished history for the last 600 years.

But there is a second way of following the route of the cross, and that is by the procession of the Veneration of the Cross. By agreeing to follow in this way, we can use it to give our assent to going with Jesus to the Father: it is Jesus who says 'Our Father', and when we say 'Our Father' with him, as sons in the Son, we are taken to God insofar as we are in Jesus. But that means we must go the way in which Christ went to the Father – the way of the cross, where he suffered because he willed it. I do not think we need to dwell on the appalling details of crucifixion; the imagination is hard to control and can absorb us into a cult of suffering. In our times, it is all too easy to realize the terribleness of torture such as the crucifixion; no one I have ever met needs to be made more appalled or more guilty. In fact, too many details of pain have a

stultifying effect, especially when we know very well
that the roots of tormenting one another are within
each of us; Christ was not crucified by someone else;
it was and is *me*. The deep root of sin is within us, and
it takes someone else to remove it. That someone is
Jesus, and it is to become part of his redeeming love
that we are here at all – it is his work; but we can at
least show willing in what is for us a costly way of
humility and simplicity, partly by agreeing to walk
and to bow down, but also by asking each other for
forgiveness: not for specific sins, but for ourselves as
we are, so much harder than condemning the distant
evils of terrorism. In the Eastern Church in Lent
everyone turns to his or her neighbour and kneels or
bows down and says, 'Forgive me' and is raised up
with the kiss of peace, and with the reply: 'Christ
between us: he is, he was, and he will be.' To be there
at all on the way to the cross, the heart must be
broken open, not broken down.

An older custom than the thirteenth-century
Stations expresses this second way of the cross, and it
was that which was seen by Egeria in Jerusalem in
394 and copied by the monks of medieval England.
In Jerusalem in the fourth century, it had recently
become possible to stand in the place of the crucifixion and to touch a part of the cross itself. In 335
Constantine's mother, Helena, with the help of
Bishop Cyril of Jerusalem (*c.* 315–386) had exca-
vated the major places of Christ's birth. Bishop Cyril
wrote, 'the saving wood of the cross was found at
Jerusalem in the time of Constantine and it was

taken fragment by fragment from this place'.[3] Much elaboration accumulated around this statement and a detailed story of the finding of the true cross was well known 50 years later, that is, by the time of Egeria. With the help of Cyril and the financial backing of her son, Helena had organized excavations in Jerusalem to find the remains of the cross and also the title and the nails.[4] These fragments were used at once to focus attention on the actuality of the cross, and it was this that Egeria saw, in Constantine's new church of the Holy Sepulchre on Good Friday. She wrote:

> The bishop's chair is placed on Golgotha behind the Cross . . . and he takes his seat. A table is placed before him with a cloth on it, the deacons stand round, and there is brought to him a gold and silver box containing the holy Wood of the Cross. It is opened, and the Wood of the Cross and the Title are taken out and placed on the table. As long as the holy Wood is on the table, the bishop sits with his hands resting on either end of it and holds it down, and the deacons round him keep watch over it. They guard it like this because what happens now is that all the people, catechumens as well as faithful, come up one by one to the table. They stoop down over it, kiss the Wood, and move on. But on one occasion (I don't know when) one of them bit off a piece of the holy Wood and stole it away, and for this reason the deacons stand round and keep watch in case anyone dares to do the

same again. Thus all the people go past one by one. They stoop down, touch the holy Wood first with their forehead and then with their eyes, and then kiss it, but no one puts out his hand to touch it. They start round about eight o'clock with everybody going by, entering by one door and going out through the other, till midday. At midday they go before the Cross, whether it is rain or fine, for the place is out of doors, into the very spacious and beautiful courtyard between the Cross and the Anastasis and there is not even room to open a door, the place is so crammed with people. They place the bishop's chair before the Cross, and the whole time between midday and three o'clock is taken up with readings. They are all about the things Jesus suffered: first the psalms on this subject, then the Apostles [the Epistles or Acts] which concern it, then passages from the Gospels. Thus they read the prophecies about what the Lord would suffer, and the Gospels about what He did suffer. And in this way they continue the readings and hymns from midday till three o'clock. It is impressive to see how all the people are moved by these readings and how they mourn. You would hardly believe how every one of them weeps during the three hours, old and young alike, because of the way in which the Lord suffered for us.[5]

The Veneration of the Cross is here followed by three hours of Bible readings. First, however, there is the visual, tactile approach of the body, touching the relic with forehead, eyes and lips, the classic method of veneration, as if saying:

> God be in my head and in my understanding;
> God be in my eyes and in my looking;
> God be in my lips and in my speaking.

Not everyone in fourth-century Jerusalem could read the account of the Passion, or understand the reflections on it by the Fathers of the Church, but everyone could do the simple thing of bowing and kissing; and they did it together in a procession. Then all gathered together for the readings in front of the cross – the Old and New Testaments together. Emotion was stirred by realization of what was done in that place, penitence brought forth. But the emphasis is not on pain or sin in itself; this adoration of the cross was not a masochistic veneration of suffering as such, but a realization that here the total agony of the world had been gathered together by Christ on the cross and therefore every suffering is healed there. For this reason, they *kiss* the cross; the significance of a kiss is of course mutual love, but it is also a sign of commitment, of agreeing in the most fleshly of all ways, with total desire, to give this pledge of accepting and being one with the redemptive act of God in Christ. But this is not automatic: there is a warning in the Gospel, for it was by a kiss that Judas greeted Christ for his betrayal; and in Jerusalem Egeria says that someone allowed personal greed to be his motivation in kissing and biting the wood of the cross. The kiss,

like all bodily actions, is in itself neutral; it must be
used with an interior intention for love. Bernard of
Clairvaux described the kiss in three stages: the kiss of
the feet signifying repentance; the kiss of the hand to
signify a desire to follow Christ; the kiss of the mouth,
a desire to be part of the love of the Trinity:[6]

> God be in my heart and in my loving.
> God be at mine end and at my departing.

In tenth-century England it was the same procession
as in Jerusalem, moving towards the kissing of the
cross, though necessarily in a more formal style.
There is here the typically English custom of 'creeping
to the cross', i.e. making three genuflections as one
goes to kiss it. The cross at Canterbury may have
contained a relic of the true cross also. This account
comes from Winchester but there was a similar ritual
in Canterbury:

> The cross shall be set up before the altar and it shall
> be held by two deacons. They shall sing *Agios O
> theos* and the lamentations . . . then unveiling the
> cross the deacons shall sing the antiphons 'Behold,
> the wood of the cross' and the verses of Fortunatus,
> 'Faithful Cross' [Venantius Fortunatus, Bishop of
> Poitiers +600; see pp. 81–2]. The abbot shall come
> before the holy cross and shall prostrate himself
> three times. Then humbly kissing the cross all the
> brethren shall do likewise.[7]

As in fourth-century Jerusalem, the ritual is of venerating the wood of the cross, by genuflections and kisses, and it was then followed by reading and chanting in its honour. The communities at Winchester and Canterbury were monks, and that provides a link with Egeria and the monks of the fourth century. But the Veneration of the Cross and the three hours of readings were not the only experience for Egeria of repentance in the desert. She also met the monks, the Desert Fathers,[8] those experts in repentance. This is the desert, the place of the 40-day withdrawal of Christ, the place of the first Christian monks. Egeria met them several times on her tour, and just before she went to Jerusalem she wrote:

We had the unexpected pleasure of seeing there (on Sinai) holy and truly dedicated monks, including some of whose reputation and holy life we had heard long before we got there. I certainly never thought I would see them, not because God would be unable to grant it, after all He has granted me everything else! But because I had heard that these monks never come in from the places where they live. We stayed two days to keep the festival of the martyr and we met the monks and they were far kinder than I deserved, greeting me warmly and having conversations. But after the feast day not a monk was to be seen. While it was still night every single one of them made off for his cell in the desert.[9]

Egeria was not really interested in what the monks had to say, and did not record it as other visitors to the desert did; if she had remembered some of their words, they would have underlined a very different way of venerating the cross, a procession undertaken in stillness, a penitential going to God as the whole of life. These were the plain men of the desert, non-liturgical, non-clerical, non-literate; alone but with the saints and angels, the friends of God, in the most basic situation for human beings – the desert. Perhaps this is the moment to pause and remember this different 'procession' by stillness rather than by walking. One of the stories told about these monastic innovators contains a phrase which typifies their way of life. Someone went to visit an old woman in the city who was renowned for sanctity; she simply stayed in her room and the visitor said, 'You idle old woman, what are you doing just sitting still?', to which she replied: 'I am not sitting still; I am on a journey.'[10] Listening to those who undertake this inner journey can be the test of external rituals: have they, by their life of stillness in the desert, chipped away or softened in any least degree the shell of self-centredness formed over the self, so that they can become a new creation with the new Adam and show in all creation the glory of the Lord? And does processional walking and kneeling do the same? Perhaps a few quotations from the world of the desert will show us something of the reality that inner procession of stillness could achieve:

Antony said, Fear not goodness as something impossible nor the pursuit of it as something alien, set a great way off; it hangs only on our own choice. For the sake of Greek learning, men go overseas, but the City of God has its foundations in every place of human habitation. The kingdom of God is within. Goodness is within us and it needs only the human heart.[11]

There were three friends and the first chose to reconcile those who were fighting against each other as it is said, 'Blessed are the peace makers'; the second chose to visit the sick; the third went to live in prayer and stillness in the desert. Now in spite of all his labours, the first could not make peace in all men's quarrels and in his sorrow he went to the one who was serving the sick and found him equally disheartened. So they went together to see the one who was living in stillness and prayer and told him their difficulties. After a short silence he poured water into a bowl and said to them, 'Look at the water', and it was disturbed. After a while he said, 'Look again', and they could see their faces reflected in the still water. Then he said, 'It is the same for those who live among men. Disturbance prevents them from seeing their faults; but when a man is still then he sees his failings.'[12]

This place was called Cellia, because of the number of cells there, scattered about in the desert. Those who have already begun their training there and want to live a more remote life, stripped of external things, withdraw there. For this is the utter desert and the cells are divided from one another by so great a distance that no one can see his neighbour, nor can any voice be heard. They live alone in their cells and there is a huge silence and a great quiet there. Only on Saturday and Sunday do they meet in church, and then they see each other face to face as men restored to heaven.[13]

Poemen said: My thought was with St Mary the Mother of God, as she wept by the cross of the Saviour. I wish that I could always weep like that.[14]

Abba Lot went to see abba Joseph and he said to him, 'Abba, as far as I can, I say my little office, I fast a little, I pray and I meditate; I live in peace and as far as I can I purify my thoughts. What else can I do?' Then the old man stood up and stretched his hands towards heaven; his fingers became like ten lamps of fire and he said to him, 'If you will, you can become all flame.'[15]

They said of Macarius that he became as it is written a god upon earth, because just as God protects the world, so Macarius would cover the faults which he saw, as though he did not see them, and those which he heard, as though he did not hear them.[16]

These glimpses of life in the solitude of the desert show another use of the body, by a stillness which is in fact journeying: 'I am not sitting still, I am on a journey.' The life of a monk is a continual procession, using the simplicities of the body, along with others. The custom of the monks was to continue to read the psalms and the other Scriptures in stillness through Easter as on all other days without any extra rituals, since they were learning the way of the crucified daily, and through their whole way of life. It is a reminder that it is not physical movement or stillness that matters in itself, but how it is linked to life in Christ. Whether in the stillness of the desert or in the processions of cathedrals, the centre of Good Friday is the cross, and in order to focus realistically on this mystery, words and actions and silence are all needed. The practice of the daily following of Christ crucified means non-judgement, silence in the face of accusation, readiness to receive the Holy Spirit, dependence on the life-giving power of God, hidden, inner sorrow rather than external weeping, knowledge of one's self in the light of God who is love. The plainness of the Desert Fathers directs us towards life and not death, to a life lived towards God and others, a true daily procession, and that is also implied in the simple bodily actions of the Good Friday procession. It is a pledge of our whole life, not just a momentary action.

Finally, I would like to look at another expression of the sense of the life-giving power of the cross. This is nowhere better expressed than in the old English poem 'The Dream of the Rood', and especially in that part of it which is carved round the edge of the Ruth-well Cross, the oldest existing High Cross.[17] Without in any way diminishing the horror of crucifixion, it is not suffering which is the focus, but the sense of the young prince who mounts the cross of pain of his own will for the cosmic act of redemption. It is there with the desert monks, in the early liturgies, on fourth-century ivories and on the Ruthwell Cross. On Palm Sunday we found a friend in a donkey; now we have a friend who is a tree. It is the tree of the cross who speaks in the poem, describing first how as a young tree it was cut down and shaped into a cross and placed ready on Golgotha:

> Unclothed Himself God Almighty when he would
>   mount the Cross,
> courageous in the sight of all men.
> I bore the powerful King, the Lord of heaven;
> I durst not bend.
> Men mocked us both together.
> I was bedewed with blood.
> Christ was on the Cross.
> Then I leaned down to the hands of men
> and they took God Almighty.[18]

Here, Christ undertakes death on the cross willingly; it is public, in the sight of all, and the wood of the tree, which can stand for our flesh, must be steady to bear it all with him. Then the tree can bend and give the body of Christ into the hands of those waiting for it, just as on Good Friday the body of Christ in the sacrament is taken and given into our hands. Self-blame is not mentioned, only the vast simplicities of the purpose of God in Christ.

There is another figure present at the cross and that is Mary. This is a reminder that the death of Christ on the cross is linked with the Annunciation – they are both the *kenosis* of the Son of God. In our processions we have had the company of many others, and especially of a donkey and a tree, and now there is also Mary, the perfect creation, the new mother of all the living, our companion at the cross. In 670 a prayer was composed by John the Archchanter, precentor at St Peter's in Rome who came to England and in 680 was teaching liturgy at the Abbey of St Peter at Wearmouth when Bede was a boy; this was his collect for 25 March, which was also celebrated sometimes on the same day as Good Friday and which therefore linked Annunciation and Passion. Here is a paraphrase of Cranmer's marvellous translation of it to express the unity of the work of redemption:

Pour your grace into our hearts we beseech thee, O Lord, that as we to whom the incarnation of Christ thy Son was made known by the message of an angel, may by his cross and passion be brought to the glory of his resurrection, who lives and reigns with you in the unity of the Holy Spirit now and for ever. Amen.[19]

Chapter 4

EASTER

The third procession is that of the Easter Vigil ceremony which is held on the night before Easter Day
and once again it is possible to come into this central
moment of the Christian year, the celebration of the
completion of salvation, by the simplest of ways, by
walking, bowing, standing, breathing, being. On
Easter night we are on even more fundamental
ground in the simplicities of this procession, which is
shaped by the basic elements of earth, of air, of fire,
and of water. There is silence at the basis of it: when
all lights in the church are extinguished, we stand
with Adam in darkness, at the moment of creation, in
earth and air only, until new light is struck out of
rock. The Scripture readings of the Vigil will later
emphasize this beginning, by using Genesis, with the
creation of all things, of which humankind is the
crown, the complete image of God. This is the time of
a new beginning, a new creation, and therefore especially it is the time of the catechumens; that is, those
who are preparing for baptism, and for those already

baptized who are with them as they go towards baptism, the unifying basis of Christian life. There is in this moment of darkness a sense of alienation, of exile, of not being at home, created in the image of God but still far off, helpless of ourselves to change. From the rock of the tomb a new light is struck from flint and shines into darkness. A candle is lit and from it small candles take their light, so that behind each small candle-flame there is the face of a human person newly made in Christ whose only identity in the darkness is that of this new light. We are taken into a new dimension of life which is pure gift. We are with the reconciled, with the baptized, with the risen Lord, who is the new Adam. It is the first and timeless day of a new creation:

> I got me flowers to straw thy way
> I got me boughs off many a tree,
> but thou wast up by break of day
> and brought'st thy sweets along with thee.
>
> Can there be any day but this,
> Though many sunnes to shine endeavour?
> We count three hundred but we miss –
> There is but one, and that one ever.[1]

This ultimate day affirms that death is no more, the last enemy is overcome, the gate of heaven is open. By simply experiencing the processions of death and life with others, we come to the last mystery – that the tomb is empty, that life rises from the tomb, that God in Christ has redeemed the world, the cross of shame is the cross of glory. Understanding it is the work of a lifetime, but because we have consented to be there, by that assent glory will permeate all we do hereafter.

> Who sweeps a room as for thy law
> makes that and the action fine.[2]

Because we agreed to walk on Palm Sunday, to bow down and kiss on Good Friday and now to stand still on Easter night, we have signified our consent through our bodies to life and death with Christ. It is not that we become good, or clever, or nice, but that we are there, ready to be loved by the love which does not depend on our actions but is a free and unconditional gift to all. It is not that we shall suddenly find ourselves totally other on Easter Day – rather we shall know that each step of ordinary living from now on is within the dynamic procession of love which is the return of Christ to the Father.

At the centre of the ceremonies on Easter night is the striking of new fire out of rock and the procession with this light to the baptismal font. Like Palm Sunday and Good Friday the earliest source for ceremonies at Easter is Jerusalem. In fourth-century Jerusalem, they did indeed strike fire from the rock of the cave-tomb, as a sign of the light which is Christ flashing out from the rock-tomb of death. Accounts say that this was done in total silence and the light carried swiftly through the city.[3] The ceremony of striking the new fire from the rock in the tomb of Christ was the origin of the New Fire Ceremonies to which was eventually added the blessing and lighting of a large beeswax candle with the new fire; this was then followed by a procession into the church, so that like the Israelites, the fire of the presence of God was seen to go before his people. By the fourth century, an elaborate hymn, the Exultet,[4] had been created in praise of the candle, explaining its significance, and stressing the exultation of all heaven and earth in the resurrection, and with the recurrent phrase, 'This is the night', centring all previous time into the present moment.

The light of the candle then fell on the page of the holy Scriptures and there were readings by its light from Old and New Testaments, telling the story from the Garden of Eden to the garden of resurrection. Another procession followed to the baptistery, the presence of all heaven being invoked with the litany of the saints, so that the whole Church, living and dead, surrounded those to be baptized, the most basic act of Christian discipleship. Then there was the blessing of the other fundamental element besides fire, the baptismal water: fire and water, basic elements of all life, were here renewed in the light of the new creation in Christ, the new Adam. The final part of the procession of Easter was for the baptized to go to the only place which remained to them on earth, the altar, to receive the life of God by physical action, eating it into themselves and therefore into the whole world.

Not all this was there in fourth-century Jerusalem. It became a more elaborate procession in time, with other elements added, but the symbolism of light and dark, of fire out of rock, Scripture readings and baptisms, of elemental renewal, was certainly there. The origins of ceremonies are always complex to trace; one of the facts about liturgy is that if it works you do it, you don't need to write it down; and this was especially true when people had really clear and accurate memories, before the invention of printing finally made us dependent on printed records. So the fact that there are few fourth-century records about details of the new fire and the baptismal rites of Easter in Jerusalem does not mean that they did not exist. Egeria wrote very briefly about Easter in Jerusalem, but her very brevity seems to suggest that such rituals were already well known in northern Europe and therefore did not need to be described to her sisters. This is what she wrote:

> They prepare for the Paschal vigil in the great church, the Martyrium; they keep the paschal vigil *like us* but there is one addition. As soon as the candidates have been baptized they are led by the bishop straight to the Anastasis where the resurrection Gospel is read. They waste no time during these services so as not to detain the people too long.[5]

Baptism was then the focus, with an extra procession after baptism for the baptized, to increase the solemnity of reading to them the resurrection Gospel. The small phrase 'like us' may suggest that the rites of Jerusalem were already well known elsewhere. As

always, Egeria has a practical note of human sympa-
thy for the physical demands of the times. It is quite
possible that the blessing and praise of the candle was
among the rites that Jerusalem and Egeria's community had in common, since the blessing of a candle
pre-dates Christianity.[6]

In medieval England they made a lot more of
Easter rituals, and occasionally wrote it all down.
There are written details from the tenth century in the
Monastic Agreement of Dunstan, citing the seventh-
century customs of Gregory the Great, the apostle of
the English, suggesting that monks for these days
should follow the baptismal customs of the cathedrals, not their own plain Scripture vigils. There are
also the details about rituals at Canterbury composed
by Archbishop Lanfranc in the eleventh century, and
these contain some of the oldest accounts of the new
fire and its procession.[7]

The *Regularis Concordia* contains this part of the
description:

Matins of Easter Eve are to be celebrated by monks
in the church of God after the manner of canons,
out of regard for the blessed Gregory, pope of the
apostolic see, as set forth in his Antiphoner.[8] The
new fire shall be brought in and the candle shall be
lit from the fire; a deacon shall bless the candle
saying the prayer '*Exultet iam angelica turba coel-
orum . . .*' Presently on a higher note he shall sing
sursum corda and the rest . . . the subdeacon shall
go to the pulpit and shall read the first lesson '*in*

principio creavit. After the readings and prayers, the litany shall be begun and the abbot shall bless the font ... *Gloria* is intoned by the master of the schola and all the lights of the church shall be lit and the bells shall peal as the abbot intones *Gloria in excelsis Deo* ...[9]

Lanfranc adds the marking of the candle with the year of the incarnation and the insertion into the wax of five grains of incense in the form of a cross.[10] He also says that in England the wise child will light a covered lantern from the new fire in case it is blown out.

So far, the English rituals reflect the rites of Jerusalem. But that was not the only visual ritual demonstration in England; for the monks, there was more to come at Matins on Easter Day itself, something visual and dramatic, with no earlier parallel:

While the third lesson is being read, four of the brethren shall vest, one of whom, wearing an alb as though for some different purpose, shall enter and go stealthily to the place of the 'sepulchre' and sit there quietly, holding a palm in his hand. Then, while the third respond is being sung, the other three brethren, vested in copes and holding thuribles in their hands, shall enter in their turn and go to the place of the 'sepulchre', step by step, as though searching for something. Now these things are done in imitation of the angel seated on the tomb and of the women coming with perfumes to anoint the body of Jesus. When, therefore, he that is seated shall see these three draw nigh, wandering about as it were and seeking some thing, he shall begin to sing softly and sweetly, 'Whom seek ye?' As soon as this has been sung right through, the three shall answer together, 'Jesus of Nazareth.' Then he that is seated shall say, 'He is not here. He is risen as he said. Go and tell them that he is risen from the dead.' At this command the three shall turn to the choir saying, 'Alleluia. The Lord is risen.' When this has been sung he that is seated, as though calling them back, shall say the antiphon, 'Come and see the place', and then, rising and lifting up the veil, he shall show them the place void of the cross and with only the linen in which the cross had been wrapped. Seeing this, the three shall lay down their thuribles in that same 'sepulchre' and, taking the linen, shall hold it up before the clergy; and, as though showing that the Lord was risen and was no longer wrapped in it, they shall sing this antiphon: 'The Lord is risen from the tomb'. They shall then lay the linen on the altar. When the antiphon is finished the prior, rejoicing in the triumph of our King in that He had conquered death and was risen, shall give out the hymn, 'We praise Thee, O God', and thereupon all the bells shall peal. After this a priest shall say the verse *Surrexit Dominus de sepulchro* right through.[11]

This is our first piece of religious drama; the texts of the Gospel have become an Easter play, based on the antiphons sung at Matins. Here are new bodily actions, a drama, a new style of procession within the liturgy, a new form for the narrative, to help contemporaries to understand and stand under. It is instructive to compare this account with the depiction of the women at the tomb from the exactly contemporary *Benedictional of St Aethelwold* (see the image on the front cover). Drama and illumination, the dynamic and plastic arts, as well as music were called in to express the theological wonder of these moments. After the walking, bowing and standing of our bodies, the impact of what God has done in Christ demands more, and it often takes the form of dialogue. The Easter texts have a kind of free, dancing delight, which is clearly expressed in an eleventh-century hymn for Easter:

> Christians to the Paschal Victim offer your
> thankful praises!
> A lamb the sheep redeemeth:
> Christ, who only is sinless,
> reconcileth sinners to the Father.
> Death and life have contended in that combat
> stupendous:
> the prince of life who died reigns immortal.
> Speak, Mary, declaring what thou sawest
> wayfaring:
> 'The tomb of Christ who is living, the glory of
> Jesus' resurrection;
> 'Bright angels attesting, the shroud and napkin
> resting.
> 'Yea, Christ my hope is arisen; to Galilee he goes
> before you.'

Christ indeed is risen, our new life obtaining;
have mercy, Victor King, ever reigning. Amen.
   Alleluia.[12]

Palm Sunday, Good Friday and Easter are not just
moments once a year; they are always here and now
and for us, not reconstructions of past events, but
truth approached through our selves as we are today.
We do not always find rejoicing easy, and especially at
Easter we need others to help us understand the true
freedom that is ours. We have found friends in these
processions – a donkey, a tree, the mother of God –
and here is another friend, perhaps the closest to us for
this last moment. Here and now in this new dawn there
is someone who weeps, broken-hearted, in a garden
and hears her name: 'Jesus saith unto her, "Mary". She
turned herself and saith unto him "Rabboni"; which is
to say, Master' (John 20.16). The young man is risen,
death is taken into victory, but it is still a time of tears,
both of sorrow and of longing and of wonder for
amazing love. It is overwhelming: as Anselm of Canterbury (1033–1109) wrote, meditating on the meeting of
this new Eve in this new garden with the new Adam:

   The Lord called her 'Mary',
   the name he had so often called her by as if to say,
   'I know who you are, and what you want;
   behold me; do not weep, I am he whom you are
      seeking.'
   At once her tears were changed;
   I do not believe they stopped at once,

but where once they were wrung from a heart
    broken and self-tormenting,
they flow now from a heart exulting.[13]

Mary of Magdala, the woman who walked in Galilee as a sinner, who bowed down uncomprehending by the cross, is now the one who stands before the Lord in the garden of new life.

Our 'procession' henceforward is always to weep with this longing which is also amazed joy, allowing ourselves to be turned towards Jesus who in the end is the only one who has called us 'friends'. In some ways it may be better to turn finally for the images for this procession of the heart not to the play of the children on a hillside, the creeping of monks to the cross, nor yet the drama of the theatre of the Church, but to stand in the stillness demanded by ultimate reality – our flesh, our body, given into the hands of God and now to be used by being still with Jesus in the life of God. We will return to these moments of procession and ritual each Sunday, each year, because though it is all done, we have to learn to believe it by living it each day. What we are learning in this basic way is in fact the highest of all theology. Behind all our processing for palms, cross and vigil, there is an eternal procession, within which we are eternally living; it is the procession of the dynamic life of the Trinity, the life shared by Father, Son and Spirit eternally; and this procession now includes all creation since Christ proceeded from the Father in the power of the Spirit into this world and returned in human nature to the

Father. This complete procession culminates in the words of the Introit for the Sunday of the Resurrection: 'I am risen and am still with Thee'.[14] These are the words of the risen Christ to the Father – the great procession from God to God is accomplished.

> In the daybreak she came, the grieving Mary,
> and summoned the other woman with her.
> Sorrowing, these two sought God's victorious Son
> alone in that earthly vault
> where they previously knew that the men of the
> Jews had hidden him.
> In the dawning there came a throng of angels,
> the rapture of those hosts surrounded the
> Saviour's tomb;
> The earthly vault was open; the Prince's corpse
> received the breath of life
> The ground shook and hell's inhabitants rejoiced;
> the young man awoke dauntless from the earth;
> the mighty Majesty arose, victorious and wise.[15]

And from this Anglo-Saxon poem, we move to Cranmer to end this chapter:

> Almighty and everlasting God, who of thy tender love towards mankind, hast sent thy Son our Saviour Jesus Christ, to take upon him our flesh, and to suffer death upon the cross, that all mankind should follow the example of his great humility: Mercifully grant, that we may both follow the example of his patience, and also be made partakers of his resurrection; through the same Jesus Christ our Lord. Amen.[16]

Chapter 5

FROM PENTECOST

The way of being in company with Christ is not limited to the moments of actual procession; it is a matter of the whole of life, whether walking or being still, alone or in company. The seventh-century English saint, Guthlac of Crowland, after a lively career as leader of a band of robbers, became a hermit and it was for his life of stillness and seclusion that he was described as '*viator Christi*',[1] one who walks with Christ. Being in company with Christ is always happening but its meaning can be highlighted at certain moments through walking, kneeling or standing. These ritual moments light up the constant state of being always with Christ:

> Christ be with me, Christ within me,
> Christ behind me, Christ before me,
> Christ beside me, Christ to win me,
> Christ to comfort and restore me.
> Christ beneath me, Christ above me,
> Christ in quiet, Christ in danger,

Christ in hearts of all that love me,
Christ in mouth of friend and stranger.[2]

All through the 50 days which end with a celebration of the first Pentecost, when the Holy Spirit descended in tongues of flame upon the expectant disciples (Acts 2.3), we continually offer ourselves to be made ready by the silent work of God, to become less self-centred, less focused upon our immediate needs, ready for the power and the wisdom of God to take over. We walk, kneel and stand; and what does God do? For the pilgrim, two things are necessary – washing and eating – and both of these can be seen as what is being done to us by Christ all the days of our journey through life. The action of being washed and given food is underlined by the ceremonies of another day during Holy Week – Maundy Thursday, the day on which two simple actions of Christ are commemorated: washing feet and giving bread at the Last Supper.

He [Jesus] riseth from supper, and laid aside his garments; and took a towel and girded himself. After that he poureth water into a bason, and began to wash the disciples' feet, and to wipe them with the towel wherewith he was girded. (John 13.4–5)

As they were eating, Jesus took bread, and blessed it, and brake it, and gave it to the disciples and said, 'Take, eat; this is my body.' (Matthew 26.26)

There are here two more simple actions: feet-washing and eating. First there is the gesture of kneeling to serve by washing dust from the feet of a neighbour: a practical necessity in a desert country when welcoming a guest, here used as a symbol of loving service of one another. This action was not repeated in Holy Week in Jerusalem in Egeria's time, and in fact the ritual belongs to the monasteries of the Middle Ages, where this custom was used each week to solemnize the work of those who served the meals. This ritual washing of feet to symbolize both service and forgiveness is given a central place in the ceremonies described in our second source, *The Monastic Agreement*. In tenth-century England in the monasteries there were two ceremonies of feet-washing: the washing of feet of the poor by the brothers and then of the brothers by the abbot:

After the mass, which shall be celebrated after Sext, there shall be assembled as many poor men as the abbot shall have provided for. Afterwards, when these have been gathered together in a suitable place, the brethren shall proceed to carry out the Maundy, at which, singing the antiphons proper to this ceremony[3] they shall wash, dry and kiss the feet of the poor men. And when water has been offered for their hands, food also shall be given to the poor men and money . . . distributed among them.[4]

After this,

> The abbot shall wash the feet of all (the brothers)
> in his own basin, drying and kissing them . . . when
> he has done this, the seniors shall minister to him
> in like manner.[5]

There can be no simpler service than to wash someone's feet; it is humble and basic, giving no glory to
the one doing it, only honouring the one washed.
It can be seen as a symbol of the daily outpouring
of mercy from God towards each of his creatures,
cleansing us from the limits and corruptions of our
own selfishness by his unfailing love. There is here also
a pattern for service to one another every day, by
mutual forgiveness and forbearance, expressed in not
judging others and giving expression to this not by
drama and emotion or any great action but by doing
the nearest and most needed job for others, however
unromantic. 'I have given you an example, that you
should do as I have done to you' (John 13.15).

But that was not the only kind of basic service
given on that evening in the upper room; there was
more offered to the 'poor' and the poor ones meant
here are all humankind, 'poor' in comparison with the
richness of God. Jesus also 'took bread and blessed it
and brake it and gave'. In order to live, people must
eat; and here the basic elements of bread and wine
were used. The Christian sacrament was not created
by external rituals like a pagan mystery; it is in itself
the person of God, who gives himself; and all that is

needed is a little bread, wine, human hands and words.

The early documents of the Christian Church, the *Didache*[6] and the *Apology* of Justin Martyr,[7] show Christians doing just this in baptism and in Eucharist; and in one of the earliest inscriptions on a Christian tomb, there is reference to Christ in both water and bread: 'Draw with a pure heart, ye mortals, from the immortal, divine spring-water; take the honey-sweet fare of the Redeemer of the saints, eat, you that are hungry.'[8]

However, there is no such account in the first source we have used, the diary of Egeria. She was writing home to her sisters about the new rituals she had observed in Jerusalem, and so she did not mention the Eucharist in detail, since that was already well established among them. For the Thursday in Holy Week she only says, 'It is the custom to assemble earlier than on ordinary days in the afternoon at the martyrium and the dismissal takes place at about four in the afternoon.'[9]

Similarly, the *Monastic Agreement* does not need to give details about the Lord's Supper which was celebrated every day; all that is said is, 'In this mass, as in those of the next two days, communion shall be given to the faithful.'[10]

As well as walking together, bowing down and standing still, we know God by the simplicities of his action towards us in washing us and feeding us. To live in company with Christ is a plain straightforward matter, always available, always effective: and a key to this is contained in the phrases 'com-pany' and 'com-panion'. '*Pan*' is derived from '*panis*', bread, and '*com*' means 'with'; 'companions' are, then, those who share bread with one another and with Christ. God, who made his creatures, knows them well and draws them to himself as they are, by means that are familiar. It is also true that each part of the way is also open to the heights of speculation and insight, and this is necessary at times, since the familiar can become either unnoticed or misunderstood. There is always more, another depth to be discovered and explored in seeking the wonder which is God, and some make this exploration more intellectually than others. But for all, the way to learn how to be more and more open to God daily can be experienced at certain moments, such as in the great processions of Holy Week; and this is re-enacted in Christian churches also in the daily procession to the altar. It was the custom from the earliest days of the Church for people to bring bread and wine forward to the altar for them to be used in the sacrament of the Eucharist. This action can be seen as another small procession, called the 'offertory'. A comparison was drawn by a great seventeenth-century preacher, Bishop Launcelot Andrewes, between this and the story told by Matthew of the 'procession' of the wise men to Bethlehem (Matthew 2.1–12), and it is not inappropriate here to recall this, since the basis of our unity with Christ is his incarnation, the beginning of his life, death and resurrection:

And now what shall we do? In the old ritual of the church we find that on the cover of the sacrament of his body there was a star engraven, to shew us that now the star leads us thither to his body there. And what shall I say but according as St John saith, and the star and the wise men, say, 'Come' and He whose the star is and to whom the wise men came saith 'Come.' And let them that are disposed come, and let whosoever will take of the bread of life which came down from heaven this day in Bethlehem the house of bread of which bread the church is this day the house, the true Bethlehem and all the Bethlehem we have now left to come to for the bread of life and this our nearest coming that here we can come until by another *venite* come unto Him in His heavenly kingdom.[11]

Pentecost, the fiftieth day, can be seen as the climax of Eastertide; Easter is the pivot of the liturgical year, not its end. There is a beginning, a preparation, a 40 days, then a time to understand (that is, to stand under) Easter, looking always towards the celebration of the gift of the Holy Spirit:

And when the day of Pentecost was fully come, they were all with one accord in one place. And suddenly there came a sound from heaven as of a rushing mighty wind, and it filled all the house where they were sitting. And there appeared unto them cloven tongues like as of fire, and it sat upon each of them. And they were all filled with the Holy

Ghost, and began to speak with other tongues, as the Spirit gave them utterance. (Acts 2.1–4)

In this mysterious passage, the images are of fire and of a wind, two of the basic elements of the world. This moment was unexpected, violent, and all those who were present could do, was accept the new power given. It was not a comfortable time; the simple, ordinary ways of humankind were taken over by the force and power of the Spirit of God, purifying, enlivening and enabling all at once. The yearly commemoration of Pentecost was traditionally, like Easter, a time for baptism, and it was therefore a beginning not an end. The processional hymns for Pentecost (see Appendix) are not about looking back to an historical event but about going onwards while at the same time remaining still, open and receptive.

The image of the breath of the Spirit has led some Christians to use their own breath as a way of praying at every moment (1 Thessalonians 5.17). Here is something even more simple, more basic to existence even than walking, kneeling, standing, eating and washing. This link between prayer and breathing is also given the form of remembering one word only, the name of 'Jesus', joined with taking breath in and out. This is a way to make prayer and company with Jesus part of every moment, alone or with others, in a cell, in a crowd, on a train, during a liturgy, walking, sitting or lying down. It is not a kind of psychosomatic technique but a way to receive always the breath of God into all our living. The Spirit of God is not a kind of pure ethereal smoke just over the top of our heads; nor is it a kind of ether just not quite tangible. It is as integral and earthy as our life as humans; breath cannot function without lungs, and the body is essential in order to be fully alive in God, and this 'breathing God' leads also to a clarification of relationship with others. These practical, simple ways of living in company with Jesus can, if we will, change us; imperceptibly we can be made more like Christ, who is total love. It is this gift of love from Christ which will unite us to one another and lead to the heavenly banquet, the supreme delight and fulfilment of all longing. This is not just for the well behaved, it is for all, and at all times. John Donne wrote about it like this:

We ask for 'daily bread' and God never says you should have come yesterday, he never says you must come again tomorrow, but today if you will hear his voice, he will hear you. God brought light out of darkness, not out of a lesser light; he can bring thy summer out of winter though thou have no spring; though in the ways of fortune or understanding or conscience thou have been benighted till now, wintered and frozen, clouded and eclypsed, damped and benummed, smothered and stupified till now, now God comes to thee, not as in the dawning of the day, not as in the bud of spring, but as the sun at noon to illustrate all shadows, as the sheaves in harvest to fill all penuries; all occasions invite his mercies and all times are his seasons.[12]

God is always *for* us, and while we recognize the seriousness of the undertaking of being in company with Christ, this does not diminish the glory and joy of the end, or prevent it from being reflected in the delights of the way itself. In any way of walking with the Lord there has to be an element, however small, of wanting somehow to go away from the old dead self and towards a fullness of life; and this has its own hardships, but the basic orientation of walking with Christ lies in a joyful sense of going out freely in good company with a shared aim, and the aim and the reward of the way is to find that place which is most of all home:

> To an open house in the evening
> Home shall men come,
> To an older place than Eden,
> And a taller town than Rome.
> To the end of the way of the wandering star,
> To the things that cannot be and that are,
> To the place where God was homeless
> And all men are at home.[13]   *Chesterton*

NOTES

Preface
1 John Wilkinson, *Egeria's Travels*, newly translated with supporting documents and notes (London, SPCK, 1971). (Hereafter *Egeria*.)
2 T. Symons (ed. and tr.), *Regularis Concordia: The Monastic Agreement of the Monks and Nuns of the English Nation* (Nelson Oxford Medieval Texts, 1953). (Hereafter *Monastic Agreement*.)
3 British Library ms add. 49598, *Benedictional of St Aethelwold*, fol. 45v.
4 G. K. Chesterton, 'The Ballad of the White Horse', in *Collected Poems of G. K. Chesterton* (London, Methuen, 1933), p. 232.

Chapter 1: The Pilgrimage of Lent
Some of the material in this chapter first appeared in *Fairacres Chronicle*, Spring 1999, Vol. 30, No. 1.
1 Augustine of Hippo, Sermon 83, for Lent.
2 John Chrysostom, Sermon for Lent.
3 Edward B. Pusey, Sermon xxix 'On Fasting', preached Lent 1, 1875.
4 Edward B. Pusey, Sermon xxix 'On Fasting', preached Lent 1, 1875.
5 Edward B. Pusey, Sermon xxviii 'On Lukewarmness', Lent 1, 1877.
6 Rupert Brooke,'Peace', in *Collected Poems* (1918).
7 *The Cloud of Unknowing*, cap. 75.
8 Venerable Bede, Sermon 1:22, 'On Lent'.
9 *Rule of St Benedict*, cap. 49.
10 Benedicta Ward (tr.), *Prayers and Meditations of Saint Anselm* (Harmondsworth, Penguin, 1973); *Letters of St Anselm*, Letter 37, 'To Lanzo'.
11 Benedicta Ward, 'Life of St Mary of Egypt', in *Harlots of the Desert* (Kalamazoo, MI, Cistercian Publications, 1987), pp. 35–56.
12 Gordon Mursell (tr.), *Meditations of Guigo* 1 (Kalamazoo, MI, Cistercian Publications, 1995), Meditation 5, p. 64.
13 *Egeria*, pp. 144–5.
14 *Egeria*, pp. 144–5.
15 *Egeria*, pp. 130–1.
16 *Monastic Agreement*, pp. 32–3.
17 *Monastic Agreement*, pp. 33–4.

18 John Bunyan, *The Pilgrim's Progress*, (London, Alexander Strahan, 1890), pp. 380ff.

Chapter 2: Palm Sunday

1 Ignatius of Antioch, 'Letter to the Romans', in *The Apostolic Fathers*, ed. and tr. Kirsopp Lake (London, Heinemann, 1919), p. 139.

2 'The Didache', in *The Apostolic Fathers*, Vol. 1, tr. Kirsopp Lake (London, Heinemann, 1919), Sections IX and X, p. 325.

3 The impact of the conversion of Constantine on the Christian Church may be readily studied in H. Chadwick, *The Church in Ancient Society* (Oxford University Press, 2004).

4 *Egeria*.

5 *Monastic Agreement*, pp. 49–50.

6 Gregory the Great, *Life of St Benedict*, tr. Caroline White, in *Early Christian Lives* (Harmondsworth, Penguin, 1998), pp. 200–1.

7 Julian of Norwich, *Revelations of Divine Love*, tr. Elizabeth Spearing (Harmondsworth, Penguin, 1998), cap. 5, p. 47.

8 *Egeria*, pp. 7–8.

9 'Eleona': Constantine's church on the Mount of Olives, cf. *Egeria*, p. 49.

10 *Egeria*, pp. 132–3.

11 Bede, *Ecclesiastical History of the English People*, ed. and tr. B. Colgrave and R. A. B. Mynors (Oxford, Clarendon Press, 1969), Book 1, cap. 25, p. 75.

12 *Monastic Agreement*, p. liv.

13 *Monastic Agreement*, pp. 34–5.

14 G. K. Chesterton, 'The Donkey', in *Collected Poems of G. K. Chesterton* (London, Methuen, 1933), p. 325.

15 Langland, *Piers Plowman*, Bk xviii.

16 Jerome, *Letter lviii to Paulinus*.

17 *Hymns Ancient and Modern*, No. 334.

Chapter 3: Good Friday

1 For a full discussion of the origins of the Stations of the Cross, see H. Thurston SJ, *The Stations of the Cross: An Account of Their History and Devotional Purpose* (London, Burns and Oates, 1906).

2 Benedicta Ward (tr.), 'A Prayer to Christ', No. 3, in *Prayers and Meditations of Saint Anselm* (Harmondsworth, Penguin, 1973), p. 95.

3 Cyril of Jerusalem, *Catechetical Lectures*, tr. J. H. Newman (1839), IV, x, p. 39.

4 For the texts and a recent discussion of the finding of the cross, see Stephan Borgehammar, *How the Holy Cross Was Found* (Stockholm, Almqvist and Wiksell International, 1991).

5 *Egeria*, p. 137.

6 Bernard of Clairvaux, *Sermons of the Song of Songs*, tr. Kilian Walsh

(Kalamazoo, MI, Cistercian Publications, 1979), Vol. 1, Sermon 3, pp. 16–20.

7 *Monastic Agreement*, pp. 42–3.

8 For an introduction to the Desert Fathers, see Rowan Williams, *Silence and Honey Cakes* (Lion Hudson, 2004).

9 *Egeria*, pp. 118–19.

10 Palladius, *Lausiac History*, tr. R. T. Meyer (London, Longmans, Green, 1965), cap. 37, p. 109.

11 Athanasius, 'Life of St Antony', in *Early Christian Lives*, tr. Caroline White (Harmondsworth, Penguin, 1998), p. 22.

12 *Wisdom of the Desert Fathers* (Oxford, SLG Press, 1975), No. 2, p. 1.

13 N. Russell (tr.), *Lives of the Desert Fathers*, with monograph by B. Ward (London, Mowbrays/Cistercian Studies, 1980), p. 149.

14 Benedicta Ward (tr.), *Sayings of the Desert Fathers: The Alphabetical Series* (London, Mowbrays/Cistercian Studies, 1975), Poemen No. 92, p. 151.

15 Benedicta Ward (tr.), *Sayings of the Desert Fathers*, Joseph No. 7, p. 88.

16 Benedicta Ward (tr.), *Sayings of the Desert Fathers*, Macarius No. 32, p. 113.

17 For a full discussion cf. Eamonn O'Carragain, *Ritual and the Rood: Liturgical Images and the Old English Poems of the* Dream of the Rood *Tradition* (London, British Library, 2005).

18 'Dream of the Rood' inscription on the Ruthwell Cross, in *Anglo Saxon Poetry*, tr. S. A. J. Bradley (London, Dent and Son, 1982), p. 2.

19 Cranmer, Collect for the Feast of the Annunciation, 25 March, in The Book of Common Prayer.

Chapter 4: Easter

1 George Herbert, *Collected Poems*, ed. F. E. Hutchinson (Oxford World Classics, 1961), 'Easter', p. 36.

2 George Herbert, *Collected Poems*, 'The Elixir', p. 175.

3 For a discussion of the origins of the Easter rituals, see A. J. McGregor, *Fire and Light in the Western Triduum* (Collegeville, MN, Liturgical Press, 1992), Chap. 13, pp. 176ff.

4 A. J. McGregor, *Fire and Light in the Western Triduum*, Chap. 28, pp. 382ff.

5 *Egeria*, p. 139.

6 A. J. McGregor, *Fire and Light in the Western Triduum*, Chap. 26, pp. 299ff.

7 A. J. McGregor, *Fire and Light in the Western Triduum*, Chap. 27, pp. 366ff.

8 This reference to Pope Gregory the Great indicates the use of cathedral rites for Easter in place of the usual Monastic Vigil.

9 *Monastic Agreement*, Chapter V, p. 49.

Notes

10 A. J. McGregor, *Fire and Light in the Western Triduum*, Chap. 21, pp. 299ff.

11 *Monastic Agreement*, pp. 49–50.

12 Jerome, Letter to Praesidius, 30, Cols. 188–9.

13 Benedicta Ward (tr.) *Prayers and Meditations of Saint Anselm* (1973), Prayer 16, 'To St Mary Magdalene', pp. 205–6.

14 Introit for the Mass of Easter Day.

15 S. A. J. Bradley (tr.), 'The Descent into Hell', in *Anglo-Saxon Poetry* (London, Dent and Son, 1982), p. 392.

16 Cranmer, Collect for the Sunday Next Before Easter, in The Book of Common Prayer.

Chapter 5: From Pentecost

1 Felix, *Life of St Guthlac of Crowland*, tr. Bertram Colgrave (Cambridge University Press, 1956), cap. xxv, p. 88, '*Viatore christo*'.

2 C. F. Alexander (tr.), 'St Patrick's Breastplate', in *English Hymnal* (1906), No. 212.

3 This is the basis of the Maundy ceremony which is still done by the Queen. It is so called from the first antiphon sung during the feet-washing, '*Mandatum novum*', 'A new commandment give I unto you' (John 13.34).

4 *Monastic Agreement*, p. 39.

5 *Monastic Agreement*, p. 40. A local addition to this ceremony is also described in the *Monastic Agreement*: 'when all are seated in refectory . . . the abbot shall go round among the brethren drinking the health and kissing the hand of each . . . then the prior shall drink to the abbot' (p. 41): an Anglo-Saxon beer-pledge custom not reflected elsewhere but suggesting that liveliness can be combined with the most solemn events.

6 'The Didache', in *The Apostolic Fathers*, Vol. 1, tr. Kirsopp Lake (London, Heinemann, 1919), Sections IX and X, pp. 323–5.

7 Justin Martyr, 'The First Apology', in *Early Christian Fathers*, Vol. 1, tr. C. C. Richardson, *et al.* (London, SCM, 1953), pp. 285–7.

8 Epitaph of Pectorius at Autun in Gaul, quoted in F. van der Meer and Christine Morhmann (eds), *Atlas of the Early Christian World* (London, Nelson, 1958), p. 42.

9 *Egeria*, 35.1, p. 134.

10 *Monastic Agreement*, 42, p. 40.

11 Launcelot Andrewes, 'Ninety Six Sermons', *Works*, Vol. 1 (Oxford, 1841), pp. 243–7.

12 John Donne, Sermon 2, in *Complete Poetry and Selected Prose*, ed. John Hayward (London, Nonesuch Press, 1929), pp. 586–7.

13 G. K. Chesterton, 'The House of Christmas', in *Collected Poems of G. K. Chesterton* (London, Methuen, 1933), p. 140.

APPENDIX OF HYMNS

1. Hymn for Lent

Guide me, O thou great Redeemer,
Pilgrim through this barren land;
I am weak but thou art mighty
Hold me with Thy powerful hand.
Bread of heaven, bread of heaven,
Feed me till I want no more.

Open now the crystal fountain,
Whence the healing stream doth flow;
Let the fire and cloudy pillar
Lead me all my journey through.
Strong Deliverer,
Be Thou still my Strength and Shield.

When I tread the verge of Jordan,
Bid my anxious fears subside;
Death of deaths, and hell's Destruction,
Land me safe on Canaan's side.
Songs of praises,
I will ever give to Thee.

(William Williams 1745,
English Hymnal (EH) 397)

Appendix of Hymns

2. Palm Sunday Hymn

All glory, laud, and honour,
To thee, Redeemer, King,
To whom the lips of children
Made sweet hosannas ring.

Thou art the King of Israel,
Thou David's royal Son,
Who in the Lord's name comest,
The King and blessèd One.

The company of angels
Are praising thee on high,
And mortal men and all things
Created make reply.

The people of the Hebrews
With palms before thee went;
Our praise and prayer and anthems
Before Thee we present.

To thee before thy passion,
They sang their hymns of praise;
To thee now high exalted,
Our melody we raise.

Thou didst accept their praises;
Accept the prayers we bring,
Who in all good delightest,
Thou good and gracious King.

(Theodulf of Orleans, *c.* 820,
trans. J. M. Neale 1851, EH 622)

3. Good Friday Hymn

The royal banners forward go;
The Cross shines forth in mystic glow;
Where he in flesh, our flesh who made,
Our sentence bore, our ransom paid:

Where deep for us the spear was dyed,
Life's torrent rushing from his side,
To wash us in that precious flood,
Where mingled Water flowed, and Blood.

Fulfilled is all that David told
In true prophetic song of old;
Amidst the nations, God, saith he,
Hath reigned and triumphed from the tree.

O Tree of beauty, Tree of light!
O Tree with royal purple dight!
Elect on whose triumphal breast
Those holy limbs should find their rest:

Blest tree, whose chosen branches bore
The wealth that did the world restore,
The price of humankind to pay,
And spoil the spoiler of his prey.

On whose dear arms, so widely flung,
The weight of this world's ransom hung:
The price of humankind to pay,
And spoil the spoiler of his prey.

O Cross, our one reliance, hail!
So may thy power with us avail
To give new virtue to the saint,
And pardon to the penitent.

To thee, eternal Three in One,
Let homage meet by all be done:
Whom by the Cross thou dost restore,
Preserve and govern evermore.

(Venantius Fortunatus, *c.* 569,
trans. J. M. Neale, 1851, EH 94
(but without verse 5))

4. Easter Hymn

Come, ye faithful, raise the strain of triumphant gladness;
God hath brought his Israel into joy from sadness;
Loosed from Pharaoh's bitter yoke, Jacob's sons and
daughters;
Led them with unmoistened foot through the Red Sea
waters.

'Tis the Spring of souls today; Christ hath burst his prison;
And from three days' sleep in death, as a Sun hath risen;
All the winter of our sins, long and dark, is flying
From his Light, to whom we give laud and praise undying.

Now the Queen of seasons, bright with the Day of
splendour,
With the royal feast of feasts, comes its joy to render;
Comes to glad Jerusalem, who with true affection
Welcomes in unwearied strains Jesu's Resurrection.

Neither might the gates of death, nor the tomb's dark
portal,
Nor the watchers, nor the seal, hold thee as a mortal;
But today amidst the twelve thou didst stand, bestowing
That thy peace which evermore passeth human knowing.

(John Damascus, *c.* 750, trans. J. M. Neale, 1851, EH 131)

5. Hymn for Pentecost

Come, thou holy Paraclete,
And from thy celestial seat
Send thy light and brilliancy:
Father of the poor, draw near;
Giver of all gifts, be here;
Come, the soul's true radiancy:

Come, of comforters the best,
Of the soul the sweetest guest,
Come in toil refreshingly:
Thou in labour rest most sweet,
Thou art shadow from the heat,
Comfort in adversity.

O thou Light, most pure and blest,
Shine within the inmost breast
Of thy faithful company.
Where thou art not, man hath nought;
Every holy deed and thought
Comes from thy Divinity.

What is soilèd, make thou pure;
What is wounded, work its cure;
What is parchèd, fructify;
What is rigid, gently bend;
What is frozen, warmly tend;
Straighten what goes erringly.

Fill thy faithful, who confide
In thy power to guard and guide;
With thy sevenfold Mystery.
Here thy grace and virtue send:
Grant salvation in the end,
And in heaven felicity.

(Anon., twelfth century,
trans. J. M. Neale, 1854, EH 155)